NORBERT NIPKIN
AND THE
MAGIC RIDDLE STONE

Design by Pamela Kinney
Cover design by Pamela Kinney

Published by Napoleon Publishing
Toronto, Ontario, Canada
www.napoleonpublishing.com
Printed in Canada

First edition printed in 1990
Second edition printed in 2000

Canadian Cataloguing in Publication Data

McConnell, G. Robert, date-
   Norbert Nipkin and the magic riddle stone

2nd ed.
ISBN 0-929141-79-2

1. Children's poetry, Canadian (English).* I. Pilcher, Steve.
II. Title.

PS8575.C644N6 2000   jC811'.54   C00-932400-3
PZ8.3.M45946No 2000

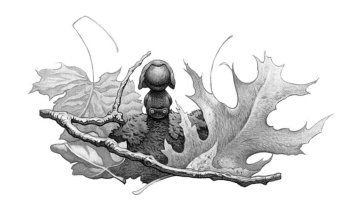

NORBERT NIPKIN

AND THE

MAGIC RIDDLE STONE

Story by
Robert McConnell

Paintings by
Steve Pilcher

Napoleon Publishing

Do you remember the story of Norbert,
The littlest Nipkin of all,
And the warning his Nanny gave him
Of the terrible dangers of fall?

When the frost is on the pumpkin,
And the leaves turn gold and red,
The soul of every Nipkin
Shudders and shivers with dread.

For this is Nipkin picking time
For the grim and gruesome Zlogs,
The heartless, pitiless giants
From the caves beyond the bogs.

They love to nibble on Nipkins
And it's such a terrible sight,
To see them munching and crunching
By the fire of a wintry night.

But sometimes when he's hunting
A hungry Zlog can't wait
For the niceties of table
And knife and fork and plate.

He'll often snatch up a Nipkin,
Then open his cavernous jaw,
And pop the tasty fellow in,
And gulp him right down raw.

Then just as Nanny had warned,
On one fateful autumn day,
The Zlogs came searching for Nipkins,
Who were impishly at play.

The Nipkins dashed for home
And never once looked back,
For there are certainly cheerier places
Than inside a Nipkin sack.

Norbert hid as best he could
But he couldn't escape a Zlog,
A boy of just about his age,
Who went by the name of Grog.

Grog hadn't eaten since breakfast;
Such hunger was hard to take,
For he'd had very little that morning —
One frog, two toads and a snake.

So he thought he'd nibble on Norbert,
Such a perfect little snack,
Then he'd get right down to the business
Of stuffing his Nipkin sack.

Just then to Grog's amazement,
To his total wonder and shock,
Norbert opened his Nipkin mouth
And lo and behold he could talk!

Both found they had so much in common,
That as it so often ends,
After less than an hour together,
Norbert and Grog were close friends.

Norbert had learnt a lesson:
Zlogs can be gentle and kind,
And Grog had made a promise
That he'd always keep in mind.

He'd never go Nipkin picking,
And he'd tell all other Zlogs
To confine their daily menus
To gartersnakes, toads and frogs.

So Grog said good-bye to Norbert
At his tiny door as planned,
Then disappeared over the hill
With a wink and wave of his hand.

THE WISH

Norbert didn't wipe his feet;
He was much too excited to bother,
For he was dying to tell his story
To his nanny, mother and father.

But before he closed the tiny door
He heard his mother cry,
"My poor little Norbert," she wailed,
"He was far too young to die!"

"He was a wonderful child," sighed father,
"And it makes me awfully sad
To think I ever raised my voice,
For he was never really bad."

"Oh, yes, I agree," nodded Nanny,
"It's a terrible trick of fate,
To realize Norbert was perfect
Just when it's all too late."

"But it's not too late!" beamed Norbert,
As he entered the room with a bound,
"There's nothing at all the matter,
I'm right here safe and sound.

"While walking today in the forest
I met the most wonderful Zlog,
I've never had a better friend —
By the way, his name is Grog.

"As a matter of fact he just left me,
Right in front of our door.
Now, isn't that tremendous?
How could you ask for more?"

Norbert's mother gasped and choked,
His father's face turned red.
Norbert was getting the feeling
He might be better dead.

"What was that I heard you say?"
His father fumed in rage,
"That's the kind of lie I'd expect
From a boy about your age!"

"Grog, indeed!" huffed Nanny,
"That's totally absurd,
It's the absolutely flimsiest
Excuse I've ever heard.

"We never could trust you, Norbert,
To listen to what we say;
You knew the Zlogs were coming
Yet you stayed outside to play."

Norbert sobbed himself to sleep
In the silence of the night,
To see how he quivered and trembled,
Was a terrible, pitiful sight.

For he dearly loved his parents,
But there was nothing he could do,
To prove he wasn't lying,
To prove his tale was true.

And when he went out next morning
It was just as he had feared;
Other children knew the story
And laughed and sneered and jeered.

"Tell us about your friend,
Tell us all about Grog,
Tell us about your adventure
With the tender-hearted Zlog!"

They gathered around little Norbert
Who felt he'd like to die,
But even though they were bigger
He was determined not to cry.

So they hemmed Norbert in with a circle,
To point and to laugh and to mock,
But they didn't have an inkling
They were in for quite a shock.

For right at that very moment
The trees began to shake,
There was an odd and eerie silence
And the earth began to quake.

"Go straight to bed!" glared Mother,
"You had us sick with worry;
There'll be no supper for you tonight,
Now off to your room and hurry!"

"But it's true!" cried little Norbert,
"Every word that I say,
I've told exactly what happened
To me in the forest today!"

"That's enough!" stared Father sternly.
"It's absurd! It can't be true!
In future no one will ever
Want to put their trust in you."

Just then a monstrous shadow
Moved to block the sun,
But when Norbert raised his saddened eyes
He knew he needn't run.

"Grog!" beamed little Norbert,
And his face showed pure delight,
But as for the other Nipkins
'Twas a classic case of fright.

"It's Grog! It's Grog!" they screamed in fear,
Their eyes bugged out, their hair on end.
"Don't eat us Grog!" they pleaded in panic,
"We're here with Norbert, he's our friend!"

They hurried and scurried and scrambled,
They bumped and they shoved and they fought,
And soon they were mangled and tangled
Into a giant Nipkin knot.

But Grog simply swept up Norb
Away from the noise and the ri
And held him gently in his han
To talk for a moment in quiet.

"I've come to say good-bye," said Grog,
"I'm running far away from home."
"But why?" asked little Norbert,
For Nipkins aren't inclined to roam.

"It's because they wouldn't believe me,
When I told them all about you,
And now they simply laugh
When I tell them it's all true.

"They claim the more I say,
The truth gets thinner and thinner,
They insist it's really absurd,
To think one can talk to one's dinner.

"When I didn't bring home any Nipkins
My parents said I was lazy,
But grandpa Zlog was sure
I'd gone absolutely crazy."

"But where will you go?" asked Norbert,
"And how will it help to leave?
There's surely nothing you can do
To make your parents believe."

"I have only one chance," whispered Grog,
"And I mean to do it alone,
The only hope I have
Is the Magic Riddle Stone."

"The Magic Riddle Stone!" gasped Norbert,
"It will be your very last breath.
You know that many have tried,
But all have met with death!

"And think where the Stone is hidden,
On top of the Mountain Morne,
Of all the places on earth
There's none more cold and forlorn.

"There are many, many dangers
You must pass along the way,
And you know the Stone is guarded
Each hour of night and day.

"And even if you find it
The riddle must be solved.
When you made this wild decision
Did you know what was involved?

"The Stone belongs to Grimald,
The Keeper of Evil and Hate.
He's guarding and hoarding its power
To conquer before it's too late."

"I know all of that," answered Grog,
"I know Grimald's plan for the earth,
But I also know of the Riddle Stone
And all the dangers it's worth.

"The Stone once had three riddles,
And a wish for the solver of each,
But there is only one riddle remaining
And the solution is hard to reach.

"But just suppose I can conquer
That Magic Riddle Stone,
Then all the power on earth
Will be mine and mine alone."

Grog looked straight at Norbert,
With sadness in his eyes,
And he seemed quite small to Norbert
Despite his massive size.

"But what would you do," queried Norbert,
"If you solved the riddle game?
Would you use your wish for power,
Or riches, glory and fame?"

"I have only one wish," sighed Grog,
"Only one goal to achieve,
When I tell my parents the truth
I just want them to believe."

"Let me come with you!" cried Norbert,
"Our wishes are really the same.
Perhaps I might even be useful,
In solving the riddle game.

"And you know how much we Nipkins
Love to be out at night.
If ever we happen to lose our way
I'll ask the fairies for light!"

"All right!" said Grog to Norbert,
"Ride on my hat, you're light as a feather,
And if we solve the riddle game
We'll share the wish together!"

And so they started their journey,
Norbert Nipkin and Grog,
To the cruel, forbidding Mountain,
Through swamp and marsh and bog.

They didn't take much with them,
Leaving at dusk in the fall,
But they knew they had each other's trust,
That most precious gift of all.

A chilling wind was wailing
As night crept o'er the land,
It slipped through field and forest
Like bones of a skeleton hand.

The moon was a sliver of ice
Pinned on the starless sky,
And Grog was becoming less certain
Of the plan he wanted to try.

Even Norbert Nipkin,
Who loved the woods at night,
Was filled with great foreboding
And a clammy feeling of fright.

A hidden, lurking power
Caused trees to moan and sway,
And it seemed a pair of ice-cold eyes
Watched every step of their way.

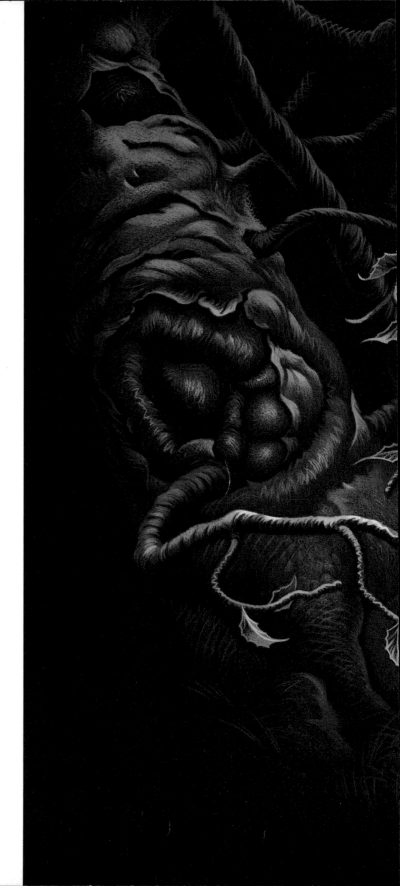

But they knew there was no turning back,
No time to regret or to grieve,
They had to conquer the Riddle Stone,
To make their parents believe.

So they stumbled along in the darkness,
As snowflakes started to fall,
But suddenly Grog stopped
And could go no further at all.

"It's the secret swamp!" stammered Norbert,
"The tales I've oft heard told
Of happenings here so gruesome
They make your blood run cold!"

"We must get across," whispered Grog,
"We must at least say we've tried.
But how can we know our direction
If we can't see the other side?"

"Marsh fairies!" gasped Norbert,
"They're coming right this way!
We can use their sparkling fairy dust
To turn the night to day.

"They must have heard our voices,
That's how they know I'm here,
They'll always help a Nipkin,
There's nothing left to fear."

So Grog slipped a log in the water
And paddled away from shore,
But even with the fairy light
He was chilled right to the core.

Further and further they paddled,
Through ferns and hanging moss,
But they sensed a pair of ice-cold eyes
Was following them across.

Suddenly, without warning,
The water boiled and churned,
There was something thrashing below them;
The log almost overturned.

A hideous, snake-like lizard,
With eyes of burning coals,
Raised its massive bulk before them
And froze their very souls.

It opened its nightmare mouth,
Its tongue forked past with a hiss,
Its teeth were an army of razors
Certain never to miss.

"The marsh monster!" stammered Norbert,
"I never thought it was true,
I was sure it was just a story
For a bedtime chill or two."

"Please forgive me Norbert,"
Grog whispered in his ear,
"I know if it weren't for me
You wouldn't now be here.

"It's a terrible way to die,
And it makes me doubly sad,
To think I've brought this horror
On the greatest friend I've had."

"It's not your fault," said Norbert,
"I wanted to come along,
I know that this is the end,
But together we'll be strong."

And so they waited together,
Norbert Nipkin and Grog,
To hear and feel those razor teeth
Crush bone and flesh and log.

They waited those horrible seconds
Frozen in fear and fright,
But in the very next instant
They were showered in brilliant light.

A thousand fairies appeared,
And then a thousand more,
Their sparkling, shimmering trails
Lit up the distant shore.

They darted round the monster's head,
They crissed and crossed his eyes,
And made him totally helpless
Despite his towering size.

Only one fairy stayed behind,
To guide the friends out of danger;
So Grog paddled swiftly away
From that ugly, red-eyed stranger.

When they were safely ashore,
They stretched out one and two,
To calm their shattered nerves,
And decide just what to do.

"That seemed like a nightmare," Grog shivered,
"Thank heavens the danger is past,
My heart was beating so hard,
I thought I'd never last.

"We'll have to wait a few hours
Until the break of day.
If we try to travel in darkness
We're sure to lose our way.

"For a moment in that swamp
I wished I'd never been born.
I hope there are no more surprises
On our way to the Mountain Morne."

He had barely uttered those words
When a shadow loomed from the night;
It was tall and swift and silent
And its face was ghostly white.

Grog stumbled back in the darkness,
He shrank from the luminous eyes
That seemed to grow in that ghostly face
And add to its frightening size.

But there was simply nowhere to go,
No place he could run and hide;
The swamp was lurking behind him
And forest on every side.

Grog felt the blood drain from his cheeks,
His head flashed cold and hot;
After all that he'd been through that night
He just fainted on the spot.

He was wakened by a soothing voice,
So rich and deep and clear,
Assuring him that he was safe
With not a thing to fear.

Grog's mouth fell open in surprise,
His bulging eyes popped out and in,
For standing there before him
Was a Zlog with a friendly grin.

He held a lantern in one hand
And in the shimmering light
An owl was perched on his shoulder
With a face of ghostly white.

"Don't be afraid of Snoot," he said,
"He's the gentlest of all souls,
The only things he fancies
Are field mice, rats and moles."

"But who are you?" asked Grog,
Peering up at that friendly face,
"I never would have believed
A Zlog could live in this place!

"What is your name? Where are you from?
And what are you doing here?
It makes me feel much safer
That a family of Zlogs is near."

"My name is Wag," said the stranger,
"And I live in this forest alone.
I know every creature that walks and flies,
Every tree and bush and stone."

"But that's not normal," said Grog,
"For a Zlog to lead such a life;
It must be awfully lonely
With no daughter, son or wife.

"You must at least have a cozy cave
To keep you warm at night,
Even with no one to talk to
In the flickering fire light."

"I don't need a cave," answered Wag,
"And I never grumble or moan,
I've never been so happy
As I am living here alone.

"I used to live with other Zlogs
Until just about your age,
But because of the way I was treated
I was filled with hate and rage.

"So finally I ran away
These many years since past,
And after horrible dangers
I reached this forest at last.

"I made friends with all the creatures
Who live among these trees,
They never laugh or mock me
And always try to please."

"But tell me why," said Grog,
"Tell me why you ran away?
Why did they laugh and mock you?
Why didn't you want to stay?"

"Let me turn round," said Wag,
With a voice both gentle and sad,
"Then you'll see why they treated me
As though I were evil and bad."

And in the glow of the lantern light
Grog saw indeed without fail
That Wag seemed perfectly normal —
Except that he had a tail.

And it wasn't a little, tiny tail,
But longish and with a bend,
And to make it more artistic
It had a tuft on the end.

"Why, it's magnificent!" cried Grog,
"It's an absolute delight!
I'm sure I've never ever seen
A more glorious, wondrous sight!"

"Do you really think so?" beamed Wag.
"It's not too long and thin?"
Then he whipped it right around
And tickled Grog on the chin.

Meanwhile Norbert Nipkin
Was keeping out of sight;
The thought of meeting a Zlog
Filled him with terrible fright.

But he was getting awfully curious
And wasn't sure what to do,
So he peeked his head up from hiding
To get a better view.

"It's a Nipkin! It's a Nipkin!"
Wag spotted him in a flash
And there was absolutely nowhere
That Norbert could dart or dash.

"I see you've brought your lunch along,
You clever little boy!
There's nothing like a Nipkin
To fill a Zlog with joy!

"It's exactly at this season
That I think about them yearly,
And lick my lips for meals long past
For oh, I love them dearly!

"Would you mind if I shared your Nipkin?
It's almost breakfast time;
To let any part of him go to waste
Would be an awful crime.

"Just let me nibble on one knee,
Or savor an elbow or two.
Why, I'd settle for a couple of toes
If you'd just remove his shoe!"

"No!" gasped Grog in horror,
"Norbert isn't a snack,
We're setting off together
To the Mountain Morne and back.

"We're going to find the Riddle Stone
To make our parents see
That Nipkins and Zlogs can be good friends
And live in harmony."

FIRE AND ICE

So Grog told Wag the whole story,
And when at last he was through,
Wag looked at them both quite kindly
And said he'd help them too.

So he told them all about Grimald,
About things they had never known,
And the stories they heard of his powers
Froze them right to the very bone.

"He has a thousand disguises,
He's the Keeper of Evil and Hate;
To fall within his spell of death
Is the most terrible, terrible fate.

"He can take the shape of anyone,
To fool and cheat and lie,
And the only way to tell
Is to look him in the eye.

"No matter what his disguise,
You know you needn't think twice,
You'll be sure you're looking at Grimald
When you see his eyes of ice.

"By now he knows of your plan
To solve the Riddle Stone,
But he wants the remaining wish
To be his and his alone.

"So he'll follow you along your way
With hateful, frozen eyes,
But he won't do a thing to stop you
Until he thinks it's wise.

"The closer you get to the Riddle Stone,
The more his power grows,
And when you can almost feel it,
That's the moment you'll be froze.

"Grimald draws power from the Stone
And if once he touches you,
You'll be frozen for eternity,
And there's nothing one can do.

"But enough of that," said Wag,
"You know you must take care;
Now the sun will soon be rising
And there's a terrible chill in the air.

"I'm going to take you home,
You need some food and rest,
You've a dangerous journey before you
And you must be at your best."

Wag's house was carved inside a tree,
And was cozy, warm and bright;
It seemed just like the perfect place
To take shelter from the night.

It was not unlike a Nipkin home,
But a thousand times the size,
With one room stacked on the other
Right up to the starry skies.

"Breakfast time!" cried Wag,
"You'll see I'm a marvelous cook.
You're going to love what I've prepared —
Just come and take a look!

"First we'll have some lizard eggs,
And I've bat-wings here to fry.
For dessert you have a choice
Of chocolate toad or spider pie."

"It sounds absolutely delicious!"
Beamed Grog as he took his place,
But poor little Norbert Nipkin
Had a sickly look on his face.

So he graciously declined
To sample that gourmet fare,
And was even so very generous
To insist Grog have his share.

Instead he took out his handkerchief
And spread each corner back,
And there were some nuts and berries and roots —
A perfect Nipkin snack.

Wag just couldn't believe his eyes,
As he munched on two crispy bat-wings;
"Surely, Norbert," he stammered in horror,
"You aren't thinking of *eating* those things!"

And when Norbert swallowed a berry,
It was almost too much for Wag,
He was sure if he didn't do something
He was going to choke and gag.

So he cut himself a double slice
Of wriggling spider pie,
And when he followed that with a chocolate toad
He gave a contented sigh.

Norbert and Grog slept most of that day
And all of the following night;
They knew they could never conquer the Stone
Without a terrible fight.

And so the very next morning,
Right at the break of day,
They packed their things together
To set out on their way.

Wag promised that he'd lead them
Past forest and rock forlorn,
Until they found the path
That led to the Mountain Morne.

But that final, fateful climb
They'd have to make alone,
They'd have to rely upon themselves
To solve the Riddle Stone.

They traveled most of the day
And didn't hear a sound,
Except for the wailing of the wind
And the swirl of snow on the ground.

But suddenly Wag stopped
And pointed dead ahead.
Norbert and Grog were filled
With a chilly feeling of dread.

"It's the Chasm of Doom," whispered Wag,
"Don't ever stray near the ledge,
There's a secret force within it
To pull you over the edge.

"They say that it goes on forever,
That is has no bottom at all,
And if you slip over that edge,
You just fall and fall and fall."

All at once they heard a sound,
A rush of air just overhead;
When they saw what was coming at them,
They thought they were surely dead.

A hideous creature was hurtling down
From a cliff as white as chalk.
It had the face of a monstrous rat
And the vicious claws of a hawk.

It was heading straight for Grog
With a sickening, hissing shriek,
It was whistling down so fast
It was barely more than a streak.

"It's an Arg! It's an Arg!" warned Wag,
"Grimald's Messenger of Hate,
Hurry and get behind me, Grog,
In a second it'll be too late!"

The Arg was larger than Wag
And it reeked of death and the tomb.
There was a furious life and death struggle
On the lip of the Chasm of Doom.

There simply seemed no way
That Wag could escape from harm;
The Arg had a claw on his throat
And the other one gripped his arm.

Norbert and Grog watched in terror
And their hearts beat faster and faster
As the Arg forced Wag to the edge,
To the very brink of disaster.

Then, in one desperate effort,
Wag's tail flashed out like a whip;
It stunned the Arg so badly
For a second it lost its grip.

And before it regained its balance,
Before it could catch its breath,
Wag wrapped his tail around it
And hurled it to its death.

But Wag was battered and bruised
As he bid his friends good-bye;
The path to Morne lay before them
Curving right up to the sky.

This was the part of the journey
They knew they must travel alone,
And they knew that Grimald was waiting,
Guarding the Magic Riddle Stone.

Before he turned back to the forest
Wag gave them some final advice —
"Grimald has a thousand disguises
But his eyes are always ice."

Norbert and Grog spent that night
In a little cave on their way;
They shivered and huddled together
Until at last it was day.

They struggled up the mountainside
Ever onward toward the sky,
They moved past rocks and twisted trees
Until the sun was high.

They saw two boulders on the path
And thought they'd catch their breath,
Before they met with Grimald
Who was plotting certain death.

So they sat down on those boulders
But they got a terrific shock,
For the boulders started moving
And then they started to talk.

When the boulders stood right up,
They had mouth and nose and eyes.
In fact they looked identical,
Only one was smaller in size.

And when they saw Norbert and Grog
They clutched each other in fear.
"Who are you?" they stammered together,
"And what are you doing here?"

"We're Norbert Nipkin and Grog.
But tell us, who are you?
We're not even shocked at talking rocks
After all that we've been through."

"He's Numb, I'm Skull; I'm Skull, he's Numb,
We're the Guardians of the Gate,
We're supposed to scare away strangers
Be it morning, noon or late."

Norbert and Grog just left them there,
Shouting and blaming each other
About who was supposed to have kept them awake —
The taller or smaller brother.

They followed the path for an hour or so,
Then turned one final bend;
"It's the top of the mountain!" gasped Norbert,
"We've reached our journey's end!"

"You don't look scary to me," said Grog,
"With twigs growing out of your ear,
You actually look quite funny,
For specialists in fright and fear."

"I'm so embarrassed!" wailed Numb,
"That you caught us in this state!
When you're funny instead of scary
That's the most terrible, terrible fate!"

And then little Skull piped up,
(He was on the verge of tears),
And said they hadn't had practice
For at least a hundred years.

THE MAGIC RIDDLE STONE

Stretched out there before them
Was a stone ledge black as coal;
A cave was at the farthest end
That they knew must be their goal.

Slowly, quietly, on they moved
Toward the Magic Riddle Stone,
But suddenly they stopped
For they knew they weren't alone.

When they took a look around them,
They felt too weak to stand,
For they saw the age-old heroes
Of Zlog and Nipkinland.

There was even Napoleon Nipkin,
With his army at his back,
Mounted on a field mouse,
Leading a Nipkin attack.

But one thing was very odd,
They didn't have to look twice —
Each of these famous heroes
Was frozen in solid ice.

Steadily onward they moved,
Norbert Nipkin and Grog,
And there by the mouth of the cave
Stood a smiling, beckoning Zlog.

"Father! Father!" cried Grog,
"I'm so terribly glad it's you!
I was sure you'd come and find me,
That you'd know my story was true!"

"No, Grog! No!" screamed Norbert,
"Stop before it's too late,
Just take a look at his eyes —
It's the Keeper of Evil and Hate!"

But in that very instant,
Quicker than one could see,
Grog was frozen in solid ice
For the rest of eternity.

But Grimald couldn't find Norbert,
Who had dashed into the cave;
Now that Grog was lost
It was himself he had to save.

And there in the cave stood the Riddle Stone —
It was massive, wide and tall;
It was a shimmering piece of granite
That formed the great side wall.

And written there upon it,
Carved in letters throbbing red,
Glowed the solitary Riddle Word
That filled Norbert's heart with dread.

EVIL was the single word
On the Magic Riddle Stone;
EVIL was the riddle
For Norbert to solve alone.

Meanwhile Norbert's family and friends
Had been searching high and low,
And when they met Wag in the forest
He showed them the way to go.

But once on the top of the Mountain,
There was simply no place to hide,
From the army of gruesome Zlogs
Who'd come up the other side.

There was Uncle, Father and Mother
And friends of Grandpa Zlog,
Who'd formed a searching party
To find their lost boy, Grog.

But when they saw the Nipkins
— Those delightful little snacks —
They wished they had remembered
To bring their Nipkin sacks.

The Nipkins darted for the cave
And scampered in like mice,
But the Zlogs just stopped in horror,
For there was Grog, in ice.

Grog's mother moaned and wailed and sobbed,
His father shed tears too,
And then he felt a tugging
On his pant down near his shoe.

And there stood little Norbert,
Frantically waving his hand.
"We must have a talk!" said Norbert,
"So that you'll understand!"

When Grog's father picked him up,
The family was in shock,
For it was just as Grog had said —
Nipkins really **could** talk!

"I'm Grog's friend," said Norbert,
"And we have no time to lose,
If we want to save Grog's life,
There is only one path to choose.

"Come into the cave," pleaded Norbert,
"We must solve the Riddle Game,
And if we cannot do it,
We have only ourselves to blame!

"But if we solve the Riddle,
We'll break the evil chain,
And use the very last wish
To make Grog breathe again.

Once they were inside the cave
Norbert introduced his father,
Who said he'd just love to help —
Of course, it would be no bother.

And although his knees were knocking
And his face was almost blue,
He added, "In such a time of crisis
It's the neighborly thing to do."

Just then there appeared before them,
Beside the Riddle glow,
A sinister, hooded figure,
In black from head to toe.

It seemed as if he had no face
To give a hint or clue,
Except that where his eyes should be
Was ice of burning blue.

"So you think you can solve my Riddle?"
His voice was black as night,
It was deep and cold and cutting,
Without a trace of light.

"I'll give you sixty seconds,
One single minute alone,
To try and steal my power
And conquer the Riddle Stone.

"But after those sixty seconds,
Your souls belong to me,
And I'll freeze your bodies in ice
For the rest of eternity."

The Nipkins and Zlogs were frantic
As they searched for another clue,
But the only word was *EVIL,*
So what could they possibly do?

"I have an idea," ventured Norbert,
"It may seem a little wild..."
But his father just said to be quiet,
This wasn't a job for a child.

And so the seconds ticked away
And the frantic search went on;
They simply were no further ahead
But thirty seconds were gone.

"I have an idea," said Norbert,
"Would you care to listen to me?"
But the adults gave him a glare
And said to leave them be.

There were only ten seconds remaining,
And then there were only five,
It seemed no Nipkin or Zlog
Would leave that cave alive.

But Norbert could wait no longer
To give his idea a try,
He ran right up to Grimald,
Despite being very shy.

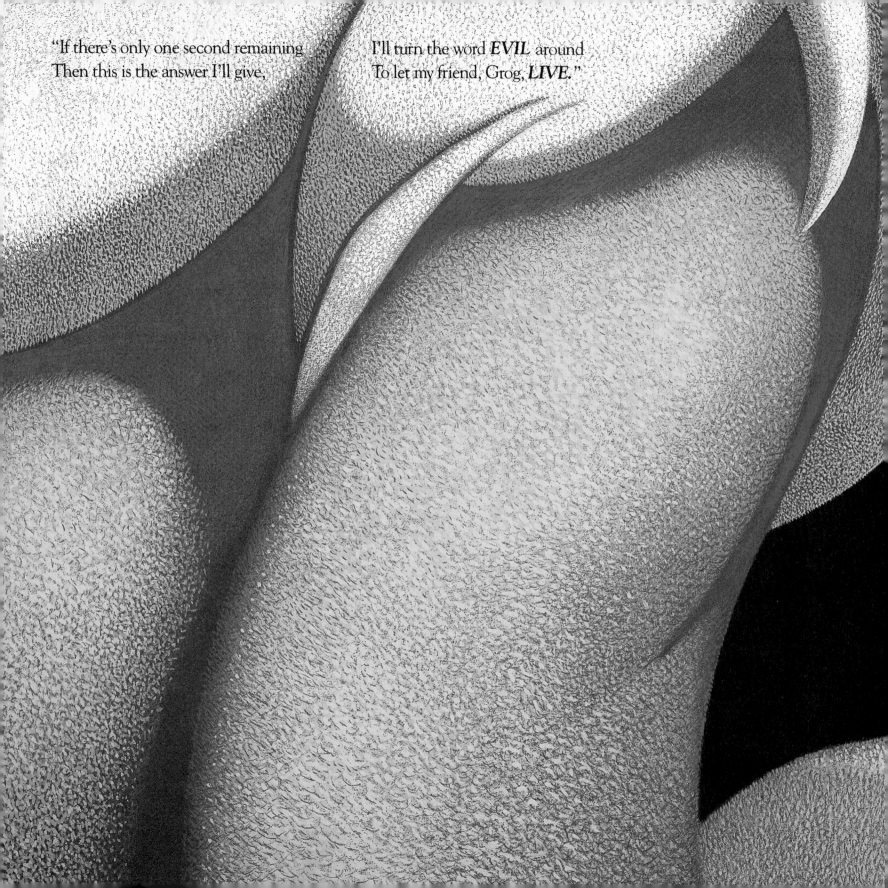

"If there's only one second remaining   I'll turn the word *EVIL* around
Then this is the answer I'll give,   To let my friend, Grog, *LIVE*."

Just at that very instant
The eyes vanished from the hood,
And a hole was burnt in the floor
Where Grimald once had stood.

And there on the wall of the cave,
On the face of the Riddle Stone,
EVIL was gone forever
And **LIVE** stood all alone.

"What's going on?" asked Grog,
As he rubbed his eyes in the light
And his mother and father rushed to his side
To hold him ever so tight.

They told him what had happened —
All that Norbert had done
To conquer the Magic Riddle Stone
And save their only son.

They introduced Norbert's parents
As their very dearest friends,
And promised what they'd do
To try and make amends.

They'd never again eat a Nipkin
And they'd tell all other Zlogs
To confine their daily menus
To gartnersnakes, toads and frogs.

And so they set off down the hill
As the waning sun grew colder,
And every Zlog had a Nipkin
Perched on his hat and his shoulder.

The meeting of strangers is funny,
It's odd how it so often ends,
After less than an hour together
It's really not hard to be friends.

The End